NIGHT LIGHT

A Story for Children Afraid of the Dark

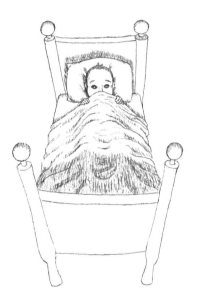

by Jack Dutro, Ph.D.

illustrated by Kenneth Boyle

MAGINATION PRESS • NEW YORK

to my daughters, Dani and Ashley, for their inspiration

Library of Congress Cataloging-in-Publication Data

Dutro, Jack.
    Night light : a story for children afraid of the dark / by Jack
Dutro : illustrated by Kenneth Boyle.
      p.   cm.
    Summary: A story of an underground child who fears the light
designed to help those who fear the dark.
    ISBN 0-945354-37-1 (hard). — ISBN 0-945354-38-X (paper)
    [1. Fear of the dark—Fiction.] I. Boyle, Kenneth, ill.
II. Title.
PZ7.D9454Ni   1991
[E]—dc20
                                           91-19612
                                                CIP
                                                AC

Published by Magination Press, an imprint of Brunner/Mazel, Inc., 19 Union Square West,
New York, NY 10003; 1-800-825-3089.

Distributed in Canada by Book Center, 1140 Beaulac St., Montreal, Quebec H4R 1R8,
Canada

Manufactured in the United States of America

10 9 8 7 6 5 4 3 2 1

Introduction for Parents

The most persistent and bothersome fears we experience are often those that have no clear threat. Fear of the dark is one of these hard-to-define and troubling problems. As parents, we know that we usually grow out of these fears. We might not know or understand how we stopped feeling frightened, but we know we did. The fear just stopped, or perhaps changed into something different.

Children do not know that the fear will stop, however. They simply know that they are afraid. *Night Light* is a creative story that taps the inner resources we use to calm our fears. Your child will use imagination to change images of fear to images of interest, fun, and comfort as the tiny creature Kalispel learns, through his experiences, to overcome his fear of light. Kalispel and his fear of light can act as a mirror to reflect insight and change and to advance your child's "growing out of" process.

The inner workings of *Night Light* are solidly based on principles of psychotherapy advanced by Milton H. Erickson. The book uses the indirect storytelling technique of a metaphor—that of representing the fear of the dark as fear of light. This reversal of light for dark and the miniature world presented are "confusion techniques," which can subtly open doors for change in a child's mind. Through paradox, Kalispel discovers that by going into the very source of his fear, the fear becomes transformed into pleasure. The behavioral and emotional matching of the main character's experiences with a child's own experiences of anxiety will help foster the unconscious development of the child's inner resources and strengths, while, at the same time, the child's conscious mind is engaged in enjoying the storyline.

While the ability to change is complex and varies from child to child, *Night Light* can provide one more spark of growth for any child.

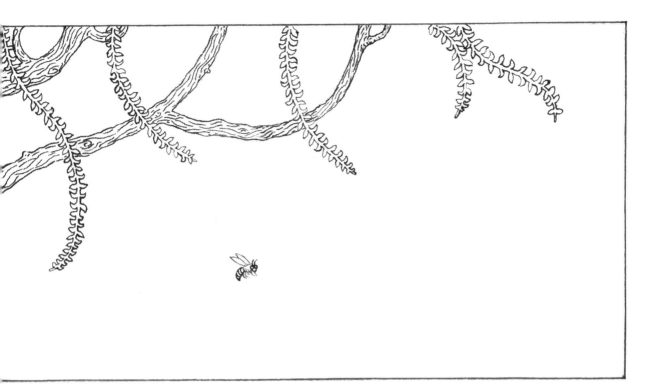

In the light of day are things you can see, like flowers dancing in a breeze or the faces in the bark of your favorite tree. In the dark underground are mysterious things. Things you may never see.

In the playground on Lincoln Street, in a corner
by a broken gate, beneath a small patch of dirt
about the size of home plate, lives a neighborhood
of tiny creatures who never see the light. In their
world, up is down, our day is their night, and
dark is their day.

When the sun sets and the light is gone, the underground creatures begin to stir. In the cool darkness of our night, which to them is day, the underground children play.

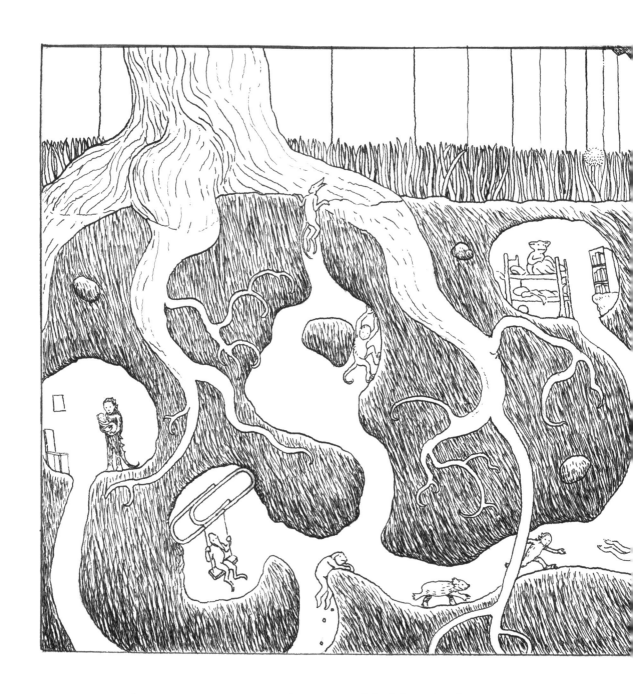

There are Rotomites, brave and bold, who love to dig. Woodlets who wait and think. Nipsies who

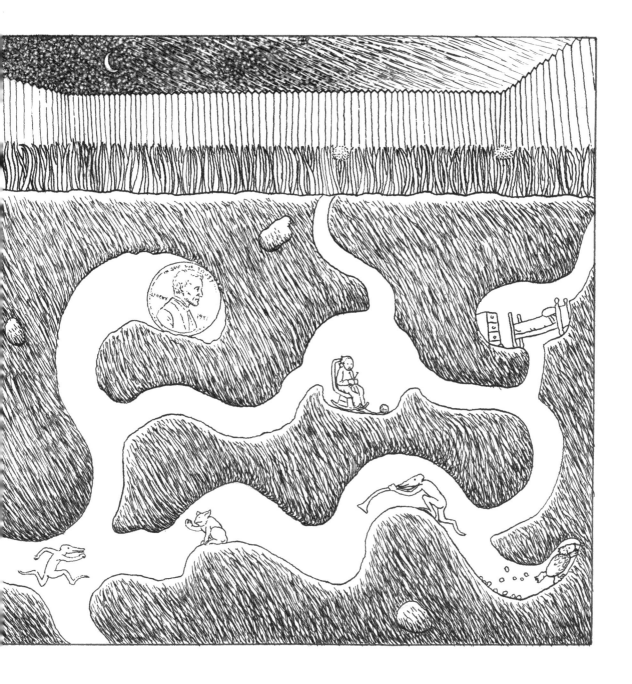

dance the underground dances and sing the silent
songs. And Thumpers who keep everyone informed.

As the sun brings morning light to wake our sleeping eyes, the tiny underground children fall asleep into their dreams.

All except for a Woodlet child named Kalispel,
who cannot go to sleep. Kalispel is afraid of
the light.

Kalispel's little room opens to an old wormhole,
where light drifts in at night. He imagines
dangerous and monstrous things that scare away
his sleep.

His mother says, "Don't be silly." His father yells,
"Just go to bed!" So Kalispel lies awake each night,
afraid of the light.

Kalispel thinks he sees something move in the wormhole. Now he is really scared. But in pops the head of his Rotomite friend.

"Digger!" Kalispel calls in relief. "What are you doing here in the light of night?"

"While digging myself to sleep, I dug into your wormhole. I came to find the light at the end of the tunnel," says Digger. "And why, Kalispel, are you awake so late?"

"You'll make fun of me," says Kalispel.

"I promise I won't," says Digger.

So Kalispel whispers, "I'm afraid of the light."

Digger remembers a fear he once had. He thinks for a minute, then he gets an idea. Bold (Rotomites are always bold) Digger tells Kalispel his plan.

Kalispel wants to wait and think, but Digger says,
"Not one more night afraid of the light." Still afraid,
Kalispel follows Digger up the old wormhole.
Together they quietly chant, "Not one more night
afraid of the light . . . Not one more night afraid of
the light."

They find the light at the end of the tunnel under
a piece of broken glass. Digger pops it out and
they step into the bright, open sunshine. The fears
Kalispel had imagined were nothing like what he
feels now.

But Kalispel follows Digger across the dirt and
through a forest of blades of grass. He looks up
and sees yellow butterflies flying in a bright blue

sky. A beetle hurries by busily gathering food. A
grasshopper jumps high over his head. Kalispel
feels like he is awake in a dream.

Finally Digger stops and says, "Here it is."

"What is it?" asks Kalispel, staring into his own
reflection.

"I don't know," says Digger, "I found it here last
night when I dug out to the light."

Now, to you and me, what they found was a
lost marble, but to Digger and Kalispel, it is an
amazing and huge crystal ball. Kalispel glows with
excitement as they push and roll the marble back
toward the old wormhole, through the forest of
grass, across the bare dirt.

Quickly Digger digs a larger opening. They roll the marble in, leaving the top open to the bright light of the night. Then they dig into the earth and the safety of the dark.

Digger starts digging again and doesn't stop until he's made a large room around the marble. The shimmering crystal ball reflects the light with a rainbow of strange and wonderful colors that fill the room with the beauty of the light of night.

"It's late, Digger," says Kalispel, "We'd better go to bed. If my mom and dad find out I went out into the light, I'll be in big trouble."

So Digger digs his way home, and Kalispel crawls under his covers.

Kalispel looks toward the wormhole and the light flowing into his room. He remembers his adventure in the light of night and the beauty of the colors in the crystal ball. Kalispel is surprised, as he closes his eyes, that the light does not scare him anymore.

In the dark of the next day, Kalispel wakes up to
the sound of voices. At the end of the wormhole he
finds Digger and almost all the children of his
neighborhood.

"They have come to see the crystal ball," says Digger.

All through the dark day the Nipsies, Woodlets,
Rotomites, and Thumpers play in the cavern
Digger had dug. They touch the smooth round
glass and look out at the moonlit sky.

Slowly comes the underground night, with the sunrise glowing bright. The room is flooded with dancing colors swirling around the walls. Everyone stares in silence at the pictures they see reflected through the crystal ball.

They marvel at the beauty of the shimmering
light until late into their night. Finally, Kalispel's
mother sends them home to their beds. "It's time
for sleep," she says.

Kalispel gazes once more into the globe of light,
into the beauty that is his night. "Good night," he
says to Digger, the brave Rotomite.

Kalispel snuggles into his bed. His mother kisses him good night and gently closes his door. He pulls the covers to his chin and looks again at the wormhole light.

"Mom!" he calls. She comes back into his room. "I'm not afraid," he says. "I left my fear in the light of the crystal ball."

On the other side of Lincoln Street, in a house
near the park, a boy named Benjamin lies awake.
He is too scared to sleep. Benjamin is afraid of
the dark.

Then Benjamin remembers a story he once heard of an underground child named Kalispel, who was afraid of the light. Benjamin smiles at the memory and breathes a big, slow sigh. Then, in some upside-down, backward kind of way, Benjamin falls asleep into the night.

Good night.

MAGINATION PRESS BOOKS

Julia, Mungo, and the Earthquake: A Story for Young People About Epilepsy
Tell Me A Story, Paint Me the Sun: When A Girl Feels Ignored by Her Father
Night Light: A Story for Children Afraid of the Dark
Putting on the Brakes: Young People's Guide to Understanding ADHD
The Potty Chronicles: A Story to Help Children Adjust to Toilet Training
Tanya and the Tobo Man: A Story in English and Spanish for Children
    Entering Therapy
Wish Upon A Star: A Story for Children With a Parent Who Is Mentally Ill
Gran-Gran's Best Trick: A Story for Children Who Have Lost Someone
    They Love
Scary Night Visitors: A Story for Children with Bedtime Fears
Ignatius Finds Help: A Story About Psychotherapy for Children
Jessica and the Wolf: A Story for Children Who Have Bad Dreams
The Blammo-Surprise! Book: A Story to Help Children Overcome Fears
Zachary's New Home: A Story for Foster and Adopted Children
Clouds and Clocks: A Story for Children Who Soil
Sammy the Elephant and Mr. Camel: A Story to Help Children
    Overcome Bedwetting
Otto Learns About His Medicine: A Story About Medication for
    Hyperactive Children
Double-Dip Feelings: Stories to Help Children Understand Emotions
This is Me and My Single Parent: A Workbook for Children and Single Parents
This is Me and My Two Families: A Workbook for Children in Stepfamilies
Cartoon Magic: How to Help Children Discover Their Rainbows Within
Robby Really Transforms: A Story About Grown-Ups Helping Children
Lizard Tales: Observations About Life